P9-API-701

Heidi

Retold by
Lisa Regan

Illustrated by
Joëlle Dreidemy

ARCTURUS

To my wonderful parents.
I love you so much.—LR.

To my dearest friend Aurore—JD.

ARCTURUS

This edition published in 2018 by Arcturus Publishing Limited
26/27 Bickels Yard, 151–153 Bermondsey Street,
London SE1 3HA

Copyright © Arcturus Holdings Limited

All rights reserved. No part of this publication may be reproduced,
stored in a retrieval system, or transmitted, in any form or by any
means, electronic, mechanical, photocopying, recording or otherwise,
without written permission in accordance with the provisions of the
Copyright Act 1956 (as amended). Any person or persons who do
any unauthorised act in relation to this publication may be liable to
criminal prosecution and civil claims for damages.

Writer: Lisa Regan
Illustrator: Joëlle Dreidemy
Designer: Jeni Child
Editor: Becca Clunes
Art Director: Jessica Crass

ISBN: 978-1-78828-684-8
CH006281NT
Supplier 24, Date 0318, Print run 6731

Printed in Malaysia

Contents

CHAPTER 1

Up the Mountain

There is a path at the foot of the mountains that winds through green meadows, past tall trees, and eventually leads the climber high into the summits, if he or she has enough breath in their lungs and energy in their legs to carry them so far.

It is on this path on a sunny morning in June that we find two figures. The first, a tall, strong-looking girl, leads the second by the hand. This character is no more than five years old, with dark curls and sunburnt skin, yet it is clear that her rosy cheeks are aglow.

It is no surprise her cheeks are alight, for this is Heidi, and she has been dressed in all the clothes she owns, despite the

summer sun. The older girl is Dete,
Heidi's aunt. She strides up the mountain
path, barely pausing as a good-natured
woman falls in step beside them.

"Is this the orphan child your sister left?"

"Yes," replied Dete. "I am taking her to
stay with Uncle."

"Are you out of your senses, Dete? He
will send you and your niece packing at
once! He speaks to no one and will never
agree to have someone live with him!"

"Nevertheless," huffed Dete, "he is her grandfather, and he must do his duty." And so, they carried on, up and up, until the little girl thought she might touch the clouds, they were so high. She ran ahead and watched for Dete to catch her up, and played happily with the goats that jumped and bleated in the grass.

As Heidi waited, she was startled by a shrill whistle. Looking about her, she spotted a thin, wiry boy marching through the mountain plants with a stick in his hand. Upon his call, the goats went hurtling in his direction, bumping and nudging his legs when they found him.

Heidi was just too hot for words. She perched on a rock and removed her clothes, until she stood only in her slip. Peter the goatherd smiled as he saw her fold the extra garments neatly, and then she climbed up next to him and asked him a thousand questions about the goats and the mountains.

Finally, Dete huffed alongside them. "Why are you undressed?" she shrieked.

"I don't want so many clothes," answered Heidi. "But I have kept them safe for you." And she pointed to the pile. Dete scooped them up and then pulled the little girl behind her.

They climbed for fifty minutes more. Eventually, they reached a small hut that stood on a rock, exposed to the winds and the sun. Behind it, the mountain rose steeply, and three old fir trees spread their shade over the roof of the dwelling.

The man that all the village called "Uncle" was sitting outside a hut, quietly looking out across the valley. Heidi

walked up to him, smiling, and put out her hand. "Good evening, Grandfather," she said politely.

"Well, well," he said gruffly. "What is the meaning of all this?" and he gazed at Heidi from beneath long, bushy eyebrows. Heidi stared back at his overgrown beard and weathered face, unable to take her eyes off him.

Dete placed a hand on Heidi's back and began to explain why she needed his help. She had looked after the girl, she said, since Heidi's parents had both passed away, but she had recently been offered an excellent job in Germany, and she must take it. Now, it was Heidi's grandfather's time to take his turn, for she had surely done more than her share in caring for the little girl.

The old man seemed to grow more angry with every word Dete said. Eventually, he shooed her back down the mountainside, where the villagers were shocked that she had left a little girl with such a grumpy old man.

Meanwhile, Heidi had begun to explore her new home. She found a lean-to shed where the goats lived when they weren't out with Peter. She listened to the sound of the breeze in the fir trees and tipped her face to the sun. Then, she retraced her steps to where the old man sat by the front door of his hut.

"What is it you want?" he asked, not unkindly.

"I want to see inside," she replied, so he stood and ducked inside the small doorway.

"Bring your clothes," he reminded her.

"I shan't need them," she said. "I want to be like the goats, with their short coats and their thin, light legs."

Grandfather studied this peculiar little girl, then smiled. He placed her clothes in a neat bundle inside a cupboard. "You may need them in the winter," he explained. The cupboard contained almost everything he owned: a change of shirt, clean underclothes, and a few plates and glasses.

"You must be hungry?" he asked. Heidi had not begun to think of food, but the question made her aware that her stomach was very empty. Grandfather laid out bread and cheese, and pulled up a stool for Heidi to sit on. Before she sat, though, she helped him set the table.

Grandfather was happy with this bright, young thing. He poured her a bowl of fresh goat's milk, which she downed thirstily. "Why, that was the tastiest milk I ever drank!" she sighed, and she tucked in to her food.

"Grandfather," she asked, when both their plates were clean. "Where shall I sleep?" His eyes flicked around the tiny hut. "Where would you like to sleep?" he asked. At once, Heidi began to explore every nook and cranny.

She climbed up a tiny ladder to the hayloft. "This would be perfect!" she declared, "I will be able to look out of the window as I fall asleep." And so, the two of them smoothed out the hay and laid a blanket on top. Heidi piled up more hay for a pillow. It looked so enticing, she could hardly wait for night to come.

And so, Heidi began her new life with Grandfather in the mountains. Every day, she would drink goat's milk for breakfast and wait for Peter to trudge up the mountainside  to add their goats to his grazing herd. She drank in the fresh, pine-scented air and the smell of the wild flowers. She petted the goats and laughed when they butted their small horns against her. Soon, she knew all their names, but Grandfather's two, called Little Bear and Little Swan, were the ones she loved the best. Before long, Grandfather trusted her enough to let her roam the mountains with Peter each day.

Heidi and Peter led the goats to the best places for them to eat fresh grasss. Heidi showed Peter how to use tasty herbs to lead the goats away from the rocky edges, where they might fall and harm their delicate bones. Grandfather always packed a large lunch for Heidi, which she shared with Peter, for she could never eat so much herself. Peter enjoyed the human company—and the lunch—and Heidi was happier than she could imagine. As the sun set each night, she gazed upon its fiery glory and then slept soundly in her little bed made of fresh hay.

CHAPTER 2
Several Visits

Summer began to fade, and the wind grew stronger, and Grandfather kept Heidi by his side on the gustiest days. He was afraid that such a tiny girl might be blown off the rocks. Instead, she stayed home and helped him make cheese, and she watched in awe as he fixed and mended and carved new furniture with all his carpenter's tools.

As winter crept in and the green of the mountains turned to white, Peter came less often. The goats huddled in their shed, and Heidi watched in excitement as thick flakes of snow drifted past the window.

On one such day, Heidi was startled by a thump at the door. Peter came in, covered

in white, and Grandfather laughed as
the heat began to thaw him out, and his
clothing trickled like a waterfall.

"So, young General," said Grandfather.
"Now that you have lost your army
of goats, you must turn to your pen
and pencil." Heidi was intrigued, and
Grandfather explained. "During the
winter, he must go to school. He needs
to learn how to read and write, but it is
tricky sometimes, am I right?"

Peter merely grunted, for he hated school. His face cheered, however, when Grandfather served him some food, for Peter's family was poor, and he was always hungry. As he finished chewing, he remembered a message.

"My grandmother would love for you to visit," he told Heidi. "As soon as the snow clears, of course," he added, seeing that Grandfather looked concerned. Heidi clapped her hands. "I cannot wait to meet your family!" she smiled.

Every day, Heidi pestered to be allowed to go down the mountain to Peter's home. Eventually, Grandfather gave in. He made Heidi dress in her warmest clothes and bundled up the little girl in a blanket. Then, they climbed onto a great wooden sleigh and set off down the mountain.

Heidi squealed with delight as they sped faster and faster down the slope. She felt as if she was flying like a bird! In no time at all, they were outside Peter's hut. Grandfather unloaded his wriggling cargo and reminded her that he would come back for her before darkness fell.

Heidi stepped from the bright sunlight into a room that seemed very dark. A woman sat at a table, mending a coat that belonged to Peter. "You must be Heidi," she said. "I am Brigitta, Peter's mother. And this is Grandmother."

Heidi walked slowly to where an old woman sat at a spinning wheel. The

woman put out her hands and grasped for Heidi's smaller ones, and then she ran her fingers over Heidi's face and hair. "You take after your mother, dear girl," she said, and she patted for Heidi to sit down beside her.

Heidi's gaze fell on a window shutter that was broken and flapping in the wind. "Why, Grandfather could fix that in no time!" she exclaimed. "And any other things that need mending. He is so kind and so clever!"

The adults exchanged glances of surprise. No one ever spoke about Uncle in that way! "Ah, my child," said the old woman. "I can hear the shutter banging and loose pieces flapping on the roof, but I cannot see them, and Peter is unable to fix such things."

Heidi could not understand how Grandmother could not see them. "Maybe if you had more light in the house, you could see?" she asked. But Grandmother sighed and said it was always dark in her eyes, no matter how bright the sun or the snow on the ground.

"But surely you can see the fire when the sun goes down?" Heidi asked, and then she burst into tears when she found out that Grandmother would never witness another glorious sunset.

A thump outside the door announced Peter's arrival home. "How was school?" asked his mother, and Peter replied sullenly, "Fine."

Grandmother gave a sigh. "Still no breakthrough with your reading, then?" she queried, and Peter grunted. Heidi wondered aloud why Peter needed to learn to read.

Grandmother took Heidi's hand again. "I have an old book of prayers and hymns," she explained, "that used to give me such pleasure. But it is so long since I heard them that I can hardly remember them. I hoped that Peter would help, but it seems to be too difficult for him."

Another thump at the door told Heidi that it was time to go. She kissed the old lady and ran out to meet her grandfather, who scooped her up and carried her home. That night, Heidi made him promise to go back to Peter's hut and repair the things that were broken. She told herself that she would visit Grandmother as often as she could.

And so, the winter passed, and Heidi made an old lady very happy. The family told the villagers all of the tasks that Uncle had done for them, and gossip began to spread that maybe he wasn't such an old grump, after all.

As spring arrived, the girl and her grandfather received a visit of their own. It was the Pastor, a serious man dressed in black. He gave Heidi such a shock when

he appeared outside, while she enjoyed
feeling the faint sun on her skin and the
new grass on her bare feet.

But Grandfather was not pleased to
see him. It was the Pastor's view that
Heidi herself was now old enough to
go to school and should certainly go
when the next winter came. He said that
Grandfather was being neglectful by not
allowing her to learn.

"She learns plenty that is useful here on the mountains with me!" Grandfather told him. "And besides, she will freeze if she has to trek to the village every day through the winter. Her mother was a sickly girl, and a sleepwalker besides. Who knows what it might do to the girl if she becomes unwell?"

"You are right," said the Pastor, "The walk to the school is too far from your mountain house. Why don't you move down into the village for the winter?"

Grandfather frowned. "No. I don't like people, and they don't like me."

And that was the end of it, as far as Grandfather was concerned. He loved Heidi but would care for her as he knew best. And that did not involve classrooms or books or reading and writing.

CHAPTER 3

New Things

Yet another visitor came to their door during that spring. Dete returned to take Heidi with her to Frankfurt. She had promised a rich family that Heidi would live with them as a companion to their sick daughter. Grandfather was not at all happy about the arrangement.

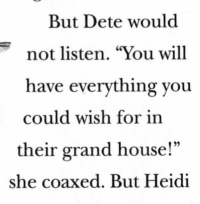

But Dete would not listen. "You will have everything you could wish for in their grand house!" she coaxed. But Heidi only wished for the mountains and the goats, the sunshine, and the chance to see Peter and Grandmother all the time.

Tears flowed down Heidi's cheeks as Dete led her down the mountainside. "Don't cry," said her aunt. "You will soon be able to come home and bring presents. Wouldn't Grandmother love some soft, white bread?"

Heidi knew that the hard, black bread was too tough for Grandmother, so she agreed that this was a good idea. She dried her eyes and hurried her steps, thinking that the sooner they arrived, the sooner she could find white bread

 and bring it back as a treat. And so, the little girl left her beloved mountain home and journeyed into the big city.

Heidi was shocked to see the house in Frankfurt. It was large, with many windows and a high roof, packed in between lots of other houses that looked much the same. Dete knocked on the grand front door, and a servant opened it. His name was Sebastian, and Heidi thought he looked very unfriendly.

He begrudgingly showed them into the hallway and left them alone. Heidi gazed at the ornate ceiling high above her. Then, a female servant, Tinette, appeared. "You had better follow me," she said curtly.

Heidi was shown into an elegant room, and Dete disappeared. A sickly looking girl lay there on the couch, covered in a blanket. She was some years older but so pale and thin that she hardly seemed any bigger than Heidi.

She introduced herself as Clara and smiled weakly at Heidi's presence. Then,

her gaze crossed the room to where a strict, cross-looking woman sat. "That is our housekeeper, Miss Rottenmeier," said Clara. The lady, who was dressed all in black, looked at Heidi from head to toe.

"So," spoke Miss Rottenmeier, "you are Heidi, are you? What kind of a name is that?" Heidi began to speak, but the lady held up a hand to stop her. "How well can you read and write? What books did you have?"

"Oh, I cannot read or write," replied Heidi. "I never had a single book. And Peter says it is very difficult to learn," she added. Clara looked at her in surprise. She had never heard anyone talk like that to Miss Rottenmeier! She smiled to herself. She was very much looking forward to having Heidi as a friend.

Heidi was given her own bedroom, and she thanked Sebastian for showing her the way. "You look so much like Peter!" she exclaimed, and the shadow of a smile crossed his face. "Child!" scolded Miss Rottenmeier. "Do not talk to the servants as if they were your friends!"

The housekeeper listed a whole host of rules that Heidi could hardly understand,

 let alone remember. Eventually, she left Heidi alone on her new bed. It was much less comfortable than her hay bed back at home. The bedroom windows were large but covered by blinds. Heidi felt like a bird that had been plucked from the skies and locked into a cage.

Life in the great house was an adventure, with all sorts of new things to understand. Clara's tutor arrived each morning to teach Heidi her ABCs, despite Heidi's fear of such things. But Heidi was easily distracted by the ways of the city, jumping up each time she heard a carriage go past or a market trader shout in the distance.

Clara was having great fun watching her new companion. Her pale cheeks gained a rosy tint, and she laughed daily at Heidi's antics. Sebastian was cheered to see his little mistress look so well, and he seldom scowled at Heidi any longer.

Heidi left the house on several occasions, and each time, Miss Rottenmeier had to send out Tinette to find her. Once, Heidi thought she heard the sound of the fir trees and ran down the road to find them. Another day, she made friends with a ragged beggar boy who took her high up in the church tower to try and see the view. Tinette had to pay him, as Heidi had promised he would receive all the coins she could find if he would only help her.

Heidi's table manners were improving, for she was quick to learn. But one night, as they ate their soup, the silence was broken by a small "Meow!" from under Heidi's chair. "What on earth is that noise?" gasped Miss Rottenmeier. Heidi lifted her new pet onto her lap.

"Get it away! Filthy animal!" cried Miss Rottenmeier. "Meow meow!" they heard again, and Heidi produced six more kittens from beneath the table. "The man was going to get rid of them," she explained, "so I said we would look after them." Miss Rottenmeier scrambled to her feet and rang the bell for Sebastian to take the kittens away.

Sebastian gave Heidi a hidden wink as he removed the seven kittens. Later, he showed her that he had tucked them safely in the kitchen and promised he would keep them out of sight when Miss Rottenmeier was prowling.

That same fierce lady called Heidi in front of her. "The only punishment I can think of for such a crime," she stated, "is to lock you in the cellar with the rats."

A cellar held no terror for Heidi. She had often gone into Grandfather's cellar, which had fresh milk, good cheese, and no rats. But Clara gasped. "Heidi did not mean to misbehave!" she exclaimed. "I will write to my father if you punish her." And so, Heidi escaped the gloom of the cellar, but it did not endear her to Miss Rottenmeier at all.

CHAPTER 4

A Ghost in the House

Clara's father, Mr. Sesemann, was often away on business, but when he came home, the mood in the house was brighter. He adored his daughter, and he was extremely happy to see the difference it made having Heidi as her friend.

"How are you getting along?" he asked Heidi, for his mind had been troubled by the tales that Miss Rottenmeier told him. Clara jumped in before Heidi could speak. "Oh, it is such fun now that Heidi is here! We have kittens, and games, and I am helping her learn her ABC."

Heidi was not so sure it was going well. She missed Grandfather and Peter, and she had been saving soft white rolls for weeks to take them back for Grandmother. She worried about the goats and missed the sight of the sun dropping behind the mountains each night.

One day, Miss Rottenmeier was putting Heidi's clean clothes in her cupboard, when she came across the bread rolls that Heidi had been setting aside. "What is the meaning of this?" she roared, then sent Tinette to find the girl.

Heidi began to explain, but Miss Rottenmeier cut her short. "I knew it! You are out of your mind!" she said unkindly and threw all of the bread rolls away. Heidi flung herself on the bed crying, until Clara became quite worried.

Eventually, she managed to calm the little girl, promising that she would get new, fresh rolls on the day that Heidi planned to visit her old home.

Miss Rottenmeier spoke to Clara's father. It was the last straw, she felt, hiding bread in the cupboard. The girl clearly had something wrong with her! But Mr. Sesemann felt otherwise.

Clara's father could see how much his daughter cared for Heidi, and he was insistent that she would be staying with them. "What is more," he stated, "I want her to be treated as an equal to Clara and looked after in every way. If she is too much for you alone," he added, "then soon, you will have extra help, for my mother is visiting next week and cannot wait to meet her."

Clara was exceedingly excited at the prospect of her grandmamma coming to stay. She told Heidi how kind and wise she was, and how she would love Heidi as much as Clara did.

Miss Rottenmeier spoke to Heidi about the visit. "You must not call her Grandmamma, but address her as Madam," she instructed. As the old lady walked up the front steps, Heidi remembered to do as she was told.

"Hello, sweet Heidi," said the lady in a very gentle voice.

"Hello, Mrs. Madam," said Heidi, trying to be polite, and everyone smiled.

"You can call me Grandmamma, just like Clara does," the lady said, and took Heidi's hand before they both pushed Clara's wheelchair into the study.

Clara's grandmother had brought presents for them all. Heidi's was a book to help with her reading, but as she turned the pages, tears sprang into her eyes. The pictures were of faraway places, from the high seas to eastern palaces, but a scene with a shepherd and his flock made Heidi feel very homesick.

She knew that Dete had hidden the truth and that she could not visit home whenever she liked. Oh, but she just wanted to see her old friends again!

Grandmother would be getting very old, and Grandfather must miss her help around the house.

Grandmamma stayed for many weeks, and Heidi's reading improved with her patience and help. But the kind lady could sense deep sadness in the little girl. Each morning, Heidi appeared at breakfast with red eyes, as if she had wept during the night.

Both Clara and Grandmamma tried to coax her to say what was wrong. But Heidi could not tell anyone, for she did not want to seem ungrateful. Eventually, Grandmamma's visit came to an end, and a sense of sadness settled over the whole house, which seemed empty without her.

Sadness was not the only emotion inside those walls. The servants muttered fearfully to each other about strange happenings that were spooking them all during the nighttime. Tinette locked her bedroom door each night. Even Miss Rottenmeier checked behind doors and kept away from dark corners and unused, empty rooms.

Each morning, the servants found the front door standing wide open. They all agreed there was a ghost in the house. They promised to keep it from Miss Clara, so that she would not be frightened and become unwell again, but they agreed that someone ought to stay awake one night to keep watch.

Sebastian was chosen to keep guard from the study next to the hall. His head drooped as midnight approached, but he stood and paced to keep himself awake. At last, in the small hours of the morning, he heard the front door creak and peeped outside his own open door.

His blood ran cold as he caught sight of a white figure standing at the top of the steps. He gulped and shook his head, and when he looked again, the figure had disappeared. The decision was made that Mr. Sesemann must be called home at once.

Clara's father returned the very next day, bringing with him his friend, the doctor. They spent some time deciding upon a course of action. That night, the pair of them waited to see what would happen. Yet again, the sound of the front door was their cue to look outside.

It was little surprise to the wise doctor to find Heidi on the doorstep. She stood

in her white nightgown, looking up and down the street. Mr. Sesemann gently scooped her up and led her inside for the doctor to examine her. They had found their little ghost!

Heidi knew nothing about her wanderings at night, for she did it in her sleep. The doctor commented how pale and sad she seemed, though. "Are you in pain? Are you happy here in Frankfurt?"

Heidi gave a small sob. Miss Rottenmeier had told her not to cry all the time, but she could not lie and pretend to be happy. "I have no pain, but a heavy feeling here inside me. And I so wish I could see the mountains again." The doctor patted her hair and looked at his friend. They both knew what she needed to be well again.

CHAPTER 5

Peter Goes to School

It was quickly decided that the doctor would take Heidi home. Heidi's parting with Clara was full of mixed emotions. Heidi loved her friend and hated to leave her, but she needed to go. They hugged each other tightly, and Mr. Sesemann promised that he and Clara would visit when Clara was well enough.

Clara made sure that Heidi had a bag of soft, white rolls for Grandmother and sweet cakes for Peter and Grandfather.

 She waved goodbye with a heavy heart. She would miss her friend.

A change had come over Grandfather while Heidi was away. He had retreated into his hermit lifestyle and no longer saw anyone in the village. But his face lit up when the girl, now grown much bigger than when he last saw her, raced toward him and flung her arms around him.

Peter's family, too, had missed her terribly. Heidi was happy to give Grandmother the bread rolls and Peter's mother the fine hat she had worn in Frankfurt.

The doctor stayed in the village for just long enough to assure himself that Heidi was happy and recovering. He checked with her Grandfather that the sleepwalking had stopped.

The doctor, however, would not leave before he extracted a promise. "Spend the worst of the winter in the village," he warned. "For the cold in that hut will surely make Heidi ill. She is still quite frail," he advised.

Then, he said his goodbyes and left them, but not without sadness of his own. In the short time he had been there, he himself had fallen in love with the fresh mountain air and the sound of the songbirds. He could not wait to return with Clara and her father the following summer.

Heidi soon settled into her old ways, eating simply, sleeping soundly, and sharing her laughter with her dearest friends. Peter often gazed at her outline as she sped ahead of him into the

sunshine, leading the goats to the best grazing ground.

Gradually, as nature would have it, the seasons changed, and the days grew colder. When the first snows fell and the ice froze in patterns like leaves on the windows, Grandfather packed up their belongings, and the pair of them moved down into the village.

Now Peter was not alone at school. Heidi dragged him to the classroom every day. He still did not think he could learn. "But Peter," she said. "If I can do it, so can you. And besides," she added naughtily, "I will tell Clara to stop sending cakes, if you do not begin to read soon."

Grandmother still loved to see Heidi, especially now that the girl could read to her from her hymn book. Her glassy eyes filled with tears as the words from her past flooded back. She squeezed Heidi's hands. "This is even better than white bread," she smiled gratefully.

Grandfather also loved to hear Heidi read, and they often sat in front of the fire together. He had patched up an old house in the village, which was too full of holes for anyone else to live in. The goats sheltered in a wooden shed, and Grandfather had even carried down Heidi's bed of hay and tucked it into a corner near the stove.

On some mornings, Heidi awoke and forgot where she was. A troubled feeling washed over her as she struggled out of bed to see if her windows had blinds again. And then, she heard the bleating of the goats and was happy once more.

The winter was long and hard, and Grandmother got sick. Heidi struggled through the snow to see her. She sent word to Clara for extra blankets and pillows to keep Grandmother warm and comfortable when she had to stay in bed.

The whole time, Grandmother did not complain. She thanked Heidi for her kindness and for keeping her soul strong with the readings from the hymn book. Heidi worried, though, for she could not visit when the weather was at its worst, and then Grandmother would not be able to hear the words she loved so much.

One evening, as Heidi sat on Grandmother's bed, and Brigitta sewed in the poor light by the fire, Peter burst into their home. "I can do it!" he cried.

"Do what?" asked his mother.

"Read," he answered, simply. And he picked up Grandmother's book and nervously began to say the words out loud. He made it through a whole hymn, and then Heidi jumped up and danced him around the room.

"Now, Grandmother can have a hymn every day, no matter whether I can come here or not!"

CHAPTER 6

Distant Friends

May had arrived, bringing its clear, warm days that tempted the flowers to show their faces. Heidi was back in her mountain home, singing happily and watching the insects as they hummed along with her.

Grandfather was extremely busy in his shed. He was making new chairs, for they were expecting important guests. "They look amazing!" exclaimed Heidi. "I can tell that one is for Grandmamma, and this one is for Clara. Oh," her face fell. "Is that one for Miss Rottenmeier? Do you think she will come?"

Peter called at that very moment, dropping the goats on his way home. He looked at the chairs and scowled.

"Oh, Peter," coaxed Heidi. "Don't worry, they are lovely people! They will love you as much as I do!" She did not tell him about Miss Rottenmeier, for she was secretly hoping that a mountain trip might be too much for the housekeeper.

But Peter and his Grandmother had secret thoughts of their own. Both were just a little bit afraid that the visitors might want to take Heidi back to the city with them when they left.

The family from Frankfurt made a strange procession when they arrived. First came two men carrying Clara in a chair. Then, another man pushed her empty wheelchair. Grandmamma rode behind them on a horse. Heidi nervously looked to see if Miss Rottenmeier was there but could not see her. Instead, she glimpsed the doctor, striding out at the back.

"Here they come!" she yelled, "and the doctor, too!" She hugged her friend, whose eyes flitted all around her, trying to take in the many sights that spread before them.

Heidi was now strong enough to push Clara around in her wheelchair, although Grandfather had other ideas. He and Peter helped Clara to her feet for a minute. At first, it hurt her legs, but gradually, she managed a little longer each day.

Clara's health improved in every aspect. Her appetite grew, her cheeks glowed, and she slept more soundly than she had ever slept in her big Frankfurt bed. She no longer trekked back down the mountain each evening, for Grandfather had convinced the doctor to let her stay in a bed that he made himself, beneath Heidi's hayloft.

Heidi took good care of her dear friend and would not leave her side. Peter tried to tempt her to the highest pastures with the goats, but Heidi said she could not. Instead, she spoke to Peter every evening, when he returned with Little Swan and Little Bear. She and Clara asked him about his days, but he barely replied. He mostly muttered, "Good evening," and continued quickly on his way.

Heidi dearly wanted to go to the highest ground, for she wanted to show Clara how beautiful it was. "Soon, you will see it for yourself," she promised.

Clara's legs grew stronger day by day, and the girls persuaded Grandfather that she was well enough to leave the hut. The old man lifted her gently from her wheelchair and strode up the mountainside as if she weighed no more than Little Swan. She beamed the whole way, until Grandfather set her down on a ledge with a view all around.

Peter was much less happy. As he strode past the hut, wishing that Clara had never come to stay, he noticed the wheelchair outside. Before he even knew what he was doing, he gave it a hard shove and sent it rocketing down the slope.

The party returned to the hut to find the chair gone and the shed door blowing in the wind. "If the chair has blown down the mountain, it will be in a hundred pieces by now," said Grandfather. He looked across to where Peter stood with the goats, hanging his head. "We must tell Mr. Sesemann what has happened."

Clara's father was planning to visit, and so they sent a message that he should bring a new chair with him. As it happened, the message did not reach him. Clara's father and grandmamma were already in the village below. It had always been their plan to visit early.

Poor Peter was certain that Grandfather knew what he had done. So, when Mr. Sesemann came striding up the mountain, the guilty boy hid behind the hut.

Of course, everyone was shocked to see them. But Clara had a surprise of her own. As her father finished greeting them all, she stood and took a few steps toward him. His eyes filled with tears, and then he turned to Grandfather. "I have heard how well you treat these girls," he said. "I am indebted to you."

"Well, Peter played his part, too," said Grandfather, with a wry smile.

Grandmamma had arrived in time to see Clara walk. She beckoned to the goatherd. "We owe you all so much," she said. "First, we took your beloved Heidi away from you. Now, you have helped our darling Clara to get well again. I know you do not want riches and city life, but will you accept our help for your families, in return for everything you have done for us?"

Peter did not know what to say, so Heidi spoke on his behalf. "As long as the help includes bread and cake, I think that will make everyone happy!"